Pig Pickin'

Moose and Hildy

Pig Pickin'

by **Stephanie Greene**
illustrated by **Joe Mathieu**

Marshall Cavendish Children

Marshall Cavendish Corporation
99 White Plains Road, Tarrytown, NY 10591
www.marshallcavendish.us

Library of Congress Cataloging-in-Publication Data

Greene, Stephanie.
Pig pickin' / by Stephanie Greene ; illustrated by Joe Mathieu.–1st ed.
p. cm. – (A Marshall Cavendish chapter book) (Moose and Hildy)
Summary: When she is invited to a "pig pickin'," Hildy believes it is a contest
to pick the prettiest pig and she hurries down south to enter, accompanied by
her good friend Moose, who soon discovers just how wrong she is.
ISBN-13: 978-0-7614-5324-6
ISBN-10: 0-7614-5324-5

[1. Pigs–Fiction. 2. Moose–Fiction. 3. Fairs–Fiction. 4. Friendship–Fiction. 5.
Humorous stories.] I. Title: Pig picking. II. Mathieu, Joseph, ill. III. Title. IV.
Series.
PZ7.G8434Pig 2006
[E]–dc22
2005037348

The text of this book is set in Garamond.
The illustrations were created with Prismacolor pencil
and Dr. Martin gray wash.

A Marshall Cavendish Chapter Book

Printed in China
First edition
2 4 6 5 3 1

Marshall Cavendish
Children

Pork barbecue is great, unless you're a pig.
—S.G.

For my grandson, Alex
—J.M.

Contents

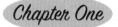

The Invitation

Moose was trimming the hedge in his garden when he heard Hildy calling him.

"I'm out back!" he shouted.

Hildy ran around the corner of the house.

"Moose!" she cried. She waved a piece of paper in the air. "The most exciting thing has happened!"

"They made the pig the state animal," said Moose. *Snip! Snip!*

"Better than that." Hildy stopped in front of him. "I've been invited to a pig pickin' down South!"

"What's a pig pickin'?" asked Moose.

"I think it's a beauty contest. You know, where they pick the prettiest pig?"

"It won't be much of a contest if you're in it," Moose said. "You'll win, hands down."

"Flatterer." Hildy swatted him with her letter.

"Where's it going to be?" Moose asked.

"Near the farm where my grandma grew up," Hildy told him. "The letter is from Wendell Hill. He's the farmer who raised Grandma. He said she was a fine figure of a pig, and he's sure I am, too."

"He's got that right."

"It sounds so exciting." Hildy's eyes were shining. "It's going to be at a county fair with games and food and rides and everything!"

"Sounds like a lot of fun."

"You will come with me, won't you?" asked Hildy. "I'm kind of nervous."

"I'll do better than that." Moose snipped the last bit of hedge. "I'll rent a car and drive us down," he said. "We'll make a vacation of it."

"Oh, Moose! You're so wonderful."

"You don't think I'd miss seeing my best friend win a beauty contest, do you?" Moose stepped back to admire his newest creation. "What do you think?"

"Who is it this time?" asked Hildy.

"General MooseArthur, the famous war hero."

"Maybe if I win the pig pickin', you'll do one of me."

"It's a deal," said Moose. "Look out, South, here we come!"

Chapter Two

The Perfect Dress

"Stop the car!" Hildy shouted.

Moose screeched to a halt on the main street of the pretty little town they had come to. "What's wrong?" he asked.

"I want that dress." Hildy pointed to the window of a small shop. A pink dress with ruffles and bows hung in the window. "I have to have that dress."

"But you packed twenty dresses," said Moose.

"I don't care." Hildy was already getting out of the car. "I know I'll win the pig pickin' if I wear that dress. Come on."

7

A bell jingled when they opened the door.

"Good morning," said the saleslady behind the counter. "What can I do for ya'll?"

"I'd like to try on the dress in the window, please," Hildy said. "Size twelve."

"I have some real pretty matching shoes . . ." said the saleslady.

"Wonderful. Size eight."

Hildy went into the dressing room to try everything on.

"Why, that dress fits you like a glove," the saleslady exclaimed when Hildy came back out. "You must be going to a wedding or something."

"Actually, I'm going to a pig pickin'."

"A pig pickin'?" The saleslady sounded surprised. "And here you are, getting all dressed up for it, too. Bless your heart."

"What does 'bless your heart' mean?" Moose asked when they were on their way again.

"I think it's the way Southerners say good luck," said Hildy.

Hmm, thought Moose. *It sounded more like 'you poor thing' to me.*

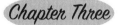

What's That Delicious Smell?

Moose and Hildy dropped off their bags at the motel and drove to the fair. A tall man was waiting for them at the entrance.

"Is that little Hildy?" he bellowed. "Why, if you aren't the spitting image of your grandma!"

"Thank you for inviting me, Mr. Hill," she said.

"None of that Mr. Hill business. You call me Wendell."

"All right, Wendell." Hildy gestured to Moose. "This is my best friend, Moose."

"We don't get many cows like you in

these parts," said Wendell.

"I'm not a cow," Moose said stiffly. "I'm a moose."

"I thought moose were big, powerful-looking animals."

"They are."

"And what about those horns they have coming out of their ears?"

"They're called antlers," Moose said. "When mine grow back this winter, they'll stretch five feet from tip to tip."

"Is that right?" Wendell said. "Then I

guess if I ever get up North, I'll know where to hang my hat."

"I think Wendell's joking," Hildy said.

"Ha-ha," said Moose.

"Sure, I'm just having some fun with you." Wendell put his arm around Hildy. "Come on, little lady. You must be hungry. Let's go get you fattened up, ah . . . I mean, get some food into you."

Moose followed them into the fair. There were people and food stands and game booths everywhere. The smell of food hung in the air like perfume.

"Mmm . . ." Hildy said when they passed a red tent with smoke billowing up from behind. "What's that delicious smell?"

"Don't worry your pretty little head," Wendell said. "Come over here and let me buy you a Belgian waffle smothered with whipped cream and strawberries."

"Oh, goody."

Hmmm, thought Moose, sniffing the air. *What is that delicious smell?*

After they ate, they rode the Ferris wheel. When they stopped at the top, they could see for miles around.

"What do you think?" Wendell asked with a sweep of his arm.

"I think it's wonderful!" cried Hildy.

"I think I'm afraid of heights," said Moose.

Next they went to the roller coaster ride. Hildy and Wendell got in line while Moose stood to the side.

"Come on, Moose!" Hildy called.

"Thanks all the same," said Moose. "But the only hills I go down are the ones where my feet can touch the ground."

The more fun Wendell showed her, the more excited Hildy got. She threw darts at balloons and baseballs at plates. She shrieked in the Haunted House and laughed in the Fun House.

In between, Wendell encouraged her to eat more.

"I'm going to burst my buttons if I keep eating like this," she said happily after a large slice of pizza.

"That's what I like to hear," said Wendell. "Another slice for the lady!"

They passed the red tent again.

"Whatever they're cooking in there sure smells delicious," Hildy said.

"How about some cotton candy?" suggested Wendell, steering her in the opposite direction.

Hmm, thought Moose. *I think I'll find out what that delicious smell is.*

19

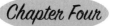

Chapter Four

The Truth about a Pig Pickin'

Moose walked over to the woman selling tickets in front of the tent.

"Excuse me," he said. "What are they cooking in there?"

"Only the best food you'll eat this side of the Mississippi," she told him.

"It does smell delicious. What is it?"

"You must not be from around these parts if you don't know Wendell Hill's Famous Pig Pickin'."

"Pig pickin'?" Moose blinked. "I thought a pig pickin' was a beauty contest."

"A beauty contest?" The lady laughed.

21

"Sorry, mister, but Wendell's Pig Pickin' is the finest barbecue in the whole state."

"Barbecue?" said Moose.

"That's right."

"What kind of barbecue?"

"Pork."

"Pork?" Moose said. "As in, pig?"

"Right again."

Moose bolted.

"What's wrong with him?" asked the next man in line.

"Beats me," said the lady. "Acts like he's never been to a pig pickin' before."

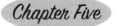
Chapter Five

Bags under Her Eyes

"Hildy!" Moose shouted as he ran up to her. "I've been looking all over for you!"

"Look what Wendell won for me," she said. She held up a stuffed animal. "Isn't it sweet?"

"Adorable." Moose started pulling her toward the gate. "Come on. We've got to get out of here."

"But Wendell's getting me an ice cream cone."

"I'll get you one on the way home."

"Home? I haven't been in the pig pickin' yet!"

"Believe me," Moose said in a low voice, "you don't want to be in the pig pickin'."

"I do, too!" Hildy planted her heels in the dirt. "And I'm not leaving here until I am."

"You're not leaving here *if* you are. You're in terrible danger!"

"What's gotten into you, Moose? You know I'm looking forward to wearing that dress."

Just then, Wendell came up to them and handed Hildy a triple-scoop cone. "What's all the whispering about?" he asked.

"Moose is trying to get me to leave," Hildy said. "He says I'm in danger."

"If you ask me, he's jealous," Wendell said smoothly. "What kind of danger could you be in at a good old county fair?"

Moose racked his brain.

"Danger of . . . I mean, danger of . . ." He got a sudden inspiration. "Danger of losing the pig pickin', Hildy!" he cried. "That's it! With all this running around, you look tired!"

"I do?"

"Tired?" Wendell protested. "Why, this girl looks good enough to eat."

Eek!

"Did you say something, Moose?" asked Hildy.

"I said, you're so tired, you've got BAGS under your eyes," he shouted.

"Bags?" Hildy patted the skin under her eyes. "Are you sure?"

"A duffel bag under each eye! Looks like you're taking a trip around the world!"

"Oh, dear. Maybe I'd better take a nap," Hildy said. "I can't go to the pig pickin' with bags under my eyes."

"Trust me," said Wendell. "No one's going to notice."

"Good idea," Moose said to her quickly, ignoring Wendell. "I'll drive you back to the motel."

"Now, hold on just one minute." Wendell stepped between them. "I'm not letting this girl out of my sight until the big event tomorrow. I'll drive you, Hildy, and I'll bring you back, too."

"Oh, Wendell. That's so sweet."

"But, Hildy . . ."

"It's all right, Moose. Wendell will take good care of me."

He'll take good care of you, all right, thought Moose as he watched them walk away. *That's what I'm afraid of.*

Chapter Six

Moose's Desperate Plan

"Quick!" Moose shouted as he ran into the dress shop. "I need another one of those dresses. Size fourteen."

The saleslady looked surprised. "But your friend wears size—"

"I know. Give me a pair of those shoes, too. Size seven."

"Good gracious!" The saleslady looked concerned. "If she's getting fatter but her feet are shrinking, she might be sick."

"I sure hope it looks that way," said Moose.

Back at the motel, Wendell was rocking

outside Hildy's door. Moose crawled in through the back window and tiptoed over to the closet. He was very careful not to wake Hildy. He took her dress off the hanger and put the new dress in its place.

He switched her shoes, too. Then he crawled back through the window.

Hildy came out of her room after her nap with a funny look on her face. "I don't understand it." She held the folds of her loose dress. "I seem to have lost some weight. And my feet are swelling up."

"Gee," Moose said nonchalantly, "I hope you're not SICK."

"Well, my feet do hurt a bit . . ."

"You look a little SICK to me," said Moose.

"Watch your language, mister," said Wendell. "No one gets sick at Wendell Hill's Pig Pickin'. Go on and change. You'll be fine after I get a few good meals into you. We can't have my prize contestant losing weight."

"Moose?" Hildy asked after she came back out. "Aren't you coming?"

"I think I'll SICK around here for awhile," said Moose. He sat down and put his feet on the railing. "I'm going to SICK back and rest my feet."

"Your friend is acting kind of funny," said Wendell.

"I think he must be jealous," said Hildy.

"Can't say that I blame him. Just looking at you makes my mouth water."

"Oh, Wendell . . ."

Great, thought Moose as they drove away. *What do I do now?*

Chapter Seven

Success!

"You again?" said the saleslady.

"Another dress," said Moose. "Size sixteen."

"Shoes, too?"

"I'm afraid so. Size six."

"Oh, dear," said the saleslady. "Have you taken her to see a doctor?"

"I'm hoping this will cure her."

Moose sneaked into Hildy's room again before she and Wendell got back from the fair. He switched her dress and shoes for the second time.

Then he went to his room and packed his bags. If this didn't work, he didn't know what he was going to do.

Bright and early the next morning, he joined Wendell outside Hildy's room.

When she finally opened her door a crack, she whispered, "Moose? Would you come in here for a minute?"

"Don't start getting shy on me, now," said Wendell. "Come on out here, Hildy. Let's see how you look."

The door creaked open. Hildy limped out.

"I don't know what happened," she said. She held her shoes in the air. "I can't even

get these on, and look at my dress! It's hanging off me."

"You don't look too good," agreed Wendell.

"This is what I was afraid of." Moose shook his head.

"What?"

"It looks to me like foot and mouth disease."

"Foot and mouth disease?" Wendell took a step back. "All we know around here

is hoof and mouth."

"Foot and mouth is what we get up North," said Moose. "From what I read in the newspapers, I believe it's spreading."

"In that case . . ." Wendell hurried over to his car. "Sorry, Hildy, but foot and mouth wasn't part of the bargain," he said as he opened the door. "I'll see you later!"

"I didn't want to go to your old pig pickin' anyway!" Moose yelled as the car screeched out of the parking lot. "I'm a vegetarian!"

"Is foot and mouth disease serious?" Hildy asked.

"Most people live with it their entire lives," said Moose.

"Then I don't understand . . ."

"Go pack your bags," said Moose. "I'll explain everything on the way home."

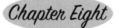
Chapter Eight

Look before You Leap

"Barbecue!" Hildy shrieked.

"The best barbecue east of the Mississippi," said Moose. He pulled onto the highway.

"You mean, I thought Wendell was being nice to me because I was pretty, but all he really wanted was to put me on a soft roll and cover me with *cole slaw*?"

"Some people like a little barbecue sauce."

"That's not funny, Moose."

"Aw, come on, Hildy. All's well that ends well."

47

"I feel so silly." Hildy shook her head. "Beauty contest. That's like a lobster thinking it's going to be judged for its pies at a lobster bake."

Moose laughed. "Or a fish for its fried chicken at a fish fry."

It was Hildy's turn to laugh.

"I'll tell you one thing," she said. "I'm going to look before I leap from now on."

"Me, too," said Moose.

They drove in silence for a while.

"Still . . ." Hildy sighed. "It would have been fun wearing a crown. I'll never get to now."

"I wouldn't be too sure about that, if I were you," said Moose.

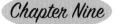

Chapter Nine

Hildy Gets Her Crown

"Where are you taking me?" Hildy asked as Moose tied the blindfold over her eyes. "What's the surprise?"

"Don't ask so many questions," he said. "Just come with me."

Moose led her around to the back of his house. He stopped in front of the hedge.

"Ta-da!" he cried. He whipped off the blindfold.

"Oh, Moose!"

Hildy stared at the dainty figure in front of her. It wore a dress with ruffles and bows, and it had on shoes to match. Best of all, on top of its head was a crown.

53

GRAND
LOSER
of
WENDELL HILL'S
World Famous
PIG PICKIN'

A great, big beautiful crown.

"Is that me?" she gasped.

"Sure is," said Moose. "Grand Loser of Wendell Hill's World Famous Pig Pickin'."

"Grand loser," Hildy said. "I never thought I'd be so happy to be called that!"